WILD LOVE

Nan Richardson &
Catherine Chermayeff
An Umbra Editions Book

WILD LOVE

CHRONICLE BOOKS

SAN FRANCISCO

Printed in Hong Kong.

Book and cover design: Vanessa Ryan
Edited by Nan Richardson and Catherine Chermayeff
Consulting Editor: Les Kaufman

Library of Congress Cataloging-in-Publication Data
Wild Love / by Nan Richardson and
Catherine Chermayeff: text by Nan Richardson.
p. cm.
ISBN 0-8118-0452-6
1. Courtship of animals--Pictorial works. I. Richardson, Nan.
II. Catherine Chermayeff
QL761.W53 1994
591.56'2'0222--dc20   93-2331
                                        CIP

Distributed in Canada by Raincoast Books,
112 East Third Avenue, Vancouver, B.C. V5T 1C8

10 9 8 7 6 5 4 3 2 1

An Umbra Editions, Inc., Book

Umbra Editions, Inc.
145 Avenue of the Americas
New York, New York 10013

Chronicle Books
275 Fifth St.
San Francisco, CA 94103

CONTENTS

INTRODUCTION

Long before Noah's ark, courtship inside the animal kingdom was as much a mystery as sex is among humankind, truly one of the mighty, irresistible instincts that dominate all living things. Three hundred million years ago, when the earth was virtually silent, lush trees rose one hundred feet to form the forest canopy, veiling streams of tropical rain and golden light. Slow-moving rivers teemed with exotic trilobites (creatures resembling horseshoe crabs). Animals began to break their bonds with the sea, and instead of simply dividing in half and cloning, sex came to be, with two creatures fusing as one. Male and female, they developed. Millennia later, we count over a million species, with possibly another million, mostly insects, remaining to be discovered. Of course, it all began when the first unicell or protozoon split in two, three billion years ago. Since then, we seem to have come a long way (for humans are composed of a hundred billion cells). In fertility, fecundity, virility, and just plain activity, protozoa may have been the superior mechanism; each cell splits into hundreds of baby cells, which become mature in a few moments and in turn split again. In fact, there are more of these invisible little "animals" than all animals combined. Meanwhile, it took better than one hundred million years for the penis and vagina to evolve, as we know them (and we might agree that it was worth the wait). It actually was the snake who initiated the quantum advance, and Adam and Eve's legend may have started there. Progressive we may be, but if every fertilized egg harks back to inherited instincts a billion years old, in each union that ancestry lives on, gaining another tiny step toward immortality. Of course, for every sperm and egg giving birth to a species, another thousand species have perished. The animals we write about here may go the way of the dodo and the brontosaurus—some 99 percent of the species that have ever lived are no more. Against that harsh reality is sex, the drive to create life. Humankind has long had a strong tendency to anthropomorphize the behavior of our fellow creatures, never more so than in their sexuality. We see ourselves in much of what animals do: tenderly paired for life, nobly defending the young to the death. But mankind also cheat on each other, or kill or maim in the course of passion. There are animal species, too, that practice rape, incest, cannibalism, and matricide. While the question—how to procreate—is the same, the answers and solutions are amazingly varied, as each year the myriad animals of the earth throw themselves whole-heartedly into the task of repopulating the earth, in the endless, effervescent arabesques of courtship and love in the wild.

The royal albatross'
overt displays of
affection continue
through their life
together, in pairings
that last as long
as twenty years.

SEMPER FIDELIS

Lifelong fidelity begins at a tender age with the royal albatross, during the first or second year of existence. At this time, though sexually immature, the albatross begins the search for a mate. After four years of ardent courtship distinguished by remarkable comradeship, an alliance is consolidated. Such permanence is essential from a biological standpoint. It takes a full year to raise a chick, and the partners take turns at extended periods of foraging for food, flying back to relieve the near-starving partner and offspring. Between broods, albatross singly cruise the ocean looking for fish. But each summer following these stints male and female both return to the nesting cliffs, to find each other again, and to remain companions during their time ashore.

Considering that twenty-four thousand pounds of hoofed flesh is involved, elephant sex is amazingly quiet and gentle.

LOVE'S WEIGHTY BURDEN

Practicing perhaps the most elemental technique for population control, the female elephant has no interest in sex during a gestation period of nearly two years, the longest of all mammals—or for the next three years spent rearing her calf. Mating twice in a decade means the moment, when it comes, must be right. The mating pair signals engagement by gentle strokings of each other's backs, twining their trunks above their heads, and a "kiss" performed by inserting their supersensitive trunks into each other's mouths. During this courtship period of elaborate foreplay, they are always inseparable: eating, sleeping, feeding, resting, and traveling. When the internal clock indicates that the day for mating has arrived (a mere three days in any cycle) the cow walks away from the herd. The bull follows, impeded by the four-foot, hundred-pound erection he drags along the ground. Then the male mounts, resting his forelegs on her back. They seem to stay perfectly still. But in fact his S-shaped penis is designed to reach far up her abdomen to her vagina, and once inserted it has a life of its own, thrusting and retreating powerfully until the climax.

The beehive swarms with sterile workers whose duties are to find and process food, while contributing to parental care of the two thousand eggs per day produced by a fertile queen. The male's role, in contrast, is limited to a nuptial flight in spring, when, with an organ analogous to a penis, the drone forces sperm directly into the queen's vaginal opening. She receives and stores the sperm in her *bursa copulatrix*, a special vault that can hold live sperm for months. For the male, this is the termination of his short life—after his task is completed he is cast from the hive. The flutter of the honeybee to the flower is an evolutionary duet choreographed by the bee's directional "waggle dance," and allows another sort of mating to take place. In exchange for sweet nectar, bees sweep from male flower to female and mate them in turn. To encourage this midwifery the flowers have their own strategies. In one extreme seduction, the bucket orchid of Central America is rigged so that the bee first falls into a tiny bucket and, climbing up the stalk to escape, is encrusted in a yellow shower, and then goes her fertile way.

One earthly society epitomizing the acme of efficiency and cooperation is run exclusively by females.

FIFTY THOUSAND VIRGINS

Hippocampus, or the sea horse of both hemispheres, has bizarre reproductive habits in which the female is the aggressor and the male the child bearer.

ROLE REVERSAL

In Greek mythology, the sea gods and river nymphs rode astride a surrealistic creature, half horse and half fish, that seemed woven from fantasy but has basis in fact. In one of the most interesting courtships in nature, the female sea horse dances around the male, then pulls him close with her prehensile tail, and they swim in a close embrace. At the right moment the male puffs up his abdomen and the female protrudes an ovipositor from her body. This "penis" is actually a prolonged genital papilla, usually of a striking orange-red hue. The female proceeds to insert it in the male's stomach pouch and thrust repeatedly, releasing, one after another, all her eggs (two hundred or more). Her multiple insertions further excite the male, who at the same time pours his sperm over the eggs. After a while the couple relinquish their embrace. The female swims off without a maternal worry in the world, while the male seals the sac with a sticky secretion and for the next four weeks travels with the eggs in his "womb," the pouch swelling like a balloon as they grow. The seeming pregnancy ends when one by one the new sea horses swim out of his body.

BIG RED BALLOON

The magnificent frigate bird, whose wingspan is wider than the height of a man, spends most of his adult life in flight, cruising high above the oceans. When a male descends from the heights to nest, he selects a tropical island and a conducive breeding area and then inflates a pouch of bright-crimson, stretchy skin in front of his throat. At the approach of a prospective female he rattles his beak against the pouch and flaps his wings, keeping up that uncomfortable dance for some time until she relents. Stiff competition between males for the few available (nonnesting) females has caused this bizzare Adam's apple, designed for cloud-level visibility, to gradually evolve.

16

The rattlesnake's
warning to rivals
becomes louder as
the snake matures,
one rattling ring
added to the tail
every year.

TWO TO TANGLE

In the animal world, conflict between potential mates is only one front of reproduction. The other battle zone is males venting aggression during the search, before the female is found. But while male competition can lead to death or severe injury, animals often use their weaponry to offer a choice: fight or flee. Striking at a speed of ten feet per second, the rattlesnake is one of the fastest killers in the animal world; rattlers resort to a combat dance for dominance instead of using their deadly venom. Raising the first third of their bodies in air, they strike rapier-fast blows until one collapses or surrenders. Keeping conflict to a minimum makes sense for the individual. Nature's etiquette often offers appeasement as alternative, and dictates that one break the opponent's spirit—not his back.

A FINE DISARRAY

Wearing yellow purple-mottled armor most of the year, the rock crab must molt in order to grow—seizing its moment of sexual opportunity.

The complex Atlantic rock crab manages to change skins by resorbing the calcium salts from the old protective shell, then swelling with water to burst out from it. Sexually mature at three or four years, the male generally molts just before mating season, to be ready and waiting for a female who happens by. He detects a faint smell, released through a chemical attractant in her urine, that tells him she is about to shed her carapace. While she slips out of her shell he holds on tight to her, helping her to disrobe. At the moment she hardens sufficiently, she allows him to insert his swimmerets (hairy minilegs on his abdomen) into her genital openings. Then she releases her thousand eggs. He, in turn, coats them with sticky sperm. Finally he relinquishes his embrace, leaving her with the egg cluster. She won't be able to mate again until the next molt.

LOVE NESTS

*The bowerbird is
a classic example
of how female
choice—once thought
unimportant in
nature—is now
understood to be
key in shaping
genetic destiny.*

Deep in the jungles of New Guinea, the male bowerbird is at work constructing a wonderland of flower petals, wallaby bones, fruit, shells, and bright leaves, all woven in elaborate nests with a pattern of dominant color. The satin bowerbird prefers blue, making a paste of blueberries that he paints on with a bark brush. For other species the recognizable element is the building style, either a maypole, teepee, pagoda, or arch. All this to entice females. In autumn, males stake out the areas between food-producing trees, constructing great edifices out of twigs. Each bird clears the canopy of leaves so that the sun lights his home and carefully weeds the vegetation at the entrance to create a stage. For the next three months the male keeps his bower fresh, changing flowers and replacing leaves daily, all the while performing periodically his mating dance. Each bower is within convenient distance of others—so the female can shop around. Once she chooses a bower, she remains until the spring, when she begins to ovulate. Upon mating she flies off to a simple nearby nest and lays her eggs. A thousand hours of work have gone into the courtship of a few minutes.

Going both ways takes on new dimensions at the bottom of the sea, where hermaphroditism is common among many species of snail.

PASSION AND PAIN

The snail or gastropod (a word that means stomach-foot in Greek), though encumbered by an attached shell several times heavier than its entire body, has a salacious sex life. While primitive forms like this jewel-top shoot sperm and eggs at each other like fireworks on the Fourth of July, many of their more modern relatives begin life as one sex and change (because of environment or convenience) to another. Mating can involve a single duet or a group including any combination of sexes. Like something from a Hieronymous Bosch tableau, a rhumba line of snails—male, female, male, female—may form, each releasing a *speculum amoris* (love dart), a chalky, spearlike substance that pierces another's skin. The wounded snail reacts with pain but also with an upsurge of passion, reciprocating with a love dart of his/her own. Together the voluptuaries lock foot-to-foot, writhing back and forth in a rhythmic frenzy. Finally spent, they lie inert for some time before they recover the strength to go their separate ways. Snails may not experience orgasm in the human sense, but these usually placid mollusks seem to have some acceptable alternative.

Among the Cichlidae,
the shimmy and
tail-beat are signs
of sexual readiness,
as the male bends
in a tight S-curve
then stretches his fins
wide, in a metaphoric
belly dance.

CASTLES IN THE SAND

Covering the sea floor with sandcastles, craters, and other architectural fantasia, the cichlids in Africa's Great Lakes are hard at work building myriad underwater platforms for mating. During the breeding season the males turn into veritable sand shovels, furiously piling up ramparts, turrets, and moats, and lakes turn into war zones of fortifications. In Lake Malawi, thousands of electrically colored males build miles of sand-castle pleasure bowers. But despite the elegant foreplay, these cichlid fathers are deadbeat dads, leaving females to shuffle off with eggs that hatch in their mouths in search of suitable nurseries in sheltered bays and rock piles.

Unlike the cartoon character of the same name, the roadrunner, especially when courting, has a lot to say.

DESERT DERVISH

One of the most remarkably adaptable birds in North America, the solar-paneled roadrunner (who can calibrate his body temperature up and down to compensate for desert sun or mountain chill) may coo, click, whine, whir, clack, growl, or bark, especially in pursuit of a mate. His vast appetite for arthropods, from tarantulas to black widow spiders, within a smorgasbord that also includes mice, bats, snails, and lizards, has a special meaning during roadrunner courtship. After hours of a dervish dance in which both male and female dash after the other, interspersed with low gliding flight, the male practices "the prance"; he throws his wings back, snaps them down to produce a popping sound, and raises and fans his tail. After this they may indulge in a little "dust-bathing," shuffling and fluttering happily in the dirt. Finally she turns away and crouches. He, dangling a plump mouse from his bill, mounts her. Copulation completed, she turns her head, tugs at the mouse, and swallows. He runs three times rapidly around her and then dashes off, at the astonishing speed (for a nine-inch bird) of twenty miles per hour.

Heavy with eggs,

the female damselfly

skirts the waves

while her consort

fends off suitors,

only too pleased

to save a damsel

from drowning.

ACROBATIC ANTICS

The damselfly's bright-winged fluttering is a courtship dance of high-wire intensity. The acutely territorial males stake out reeds or twigs around a pond, where—tails up and wings spread wide—they threaten interlopers who fly too close. The male proffers his sheltered site as a bribe to persuade a female to join him, displaying his physique to aerial female traffic. If a tempted female lands he courts her by hovering in front, then grasps her behind with special claspers at the end of his abdomen. This posture puts his genital opening above her head (where she can't possibly reach it), so he performs a Herculean feat, lifting the female aloft while she brings her abdomen forward to complete a mating "ring." Then the male inserts a peculiarly hook-shaped organ and cleans her genital tract. He gently rocks up and down for a minute or two as he swabs, finally releasing sperm into the pristine womb. With her own sharp-edged egg-laying tool, at the tip of her abdomen, the female will soon cut tiny holes in the stems of aquatic plants to push a single egg into each. If another male seizes her at this point, his very first act will be to rid her of his predecessor's sperm.

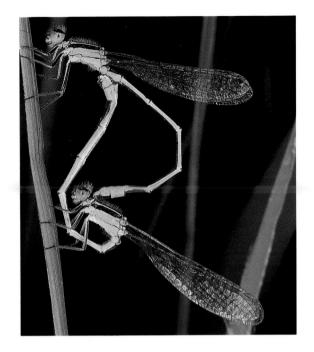

The Great egret's long elegant body with graceful neck, bright lime-green feathers around the eyes, and crowning aigrette make it among the most beautiful of birds, especially in their mating plumage. Courtship begins as, side by side, wings folded and necks stretched, the egrets utter rapid, throaty, low-pitched cuk-cuk cries. After claiming a nesting site (often involving squabbles with other males), a male waits for courting females to come to him. Unsuitable females are driven away after a kind of aerial joust in which, held aloft by a stiff breeze, the two egrets lunge at each other. He may joust with half a dozen females before selecting a mate. The two then settle down to nest building, but when she departs for several days of foraging before laying her eggs he resumes his courting ritual. He doesn't, however, actually choose another mate unless his first fails to return—a kind of "divorce insurance," as one ornithologist dubbed it.

The egret's spotless nuptial train, sporting feathers up to fifty-four inches long, is grown in spring and gone by summer when courtship is concluded.

CROWNING GLORIES

JAWS OF DESIRE

Crocodilian courtship is a leisurely affair that may last several days, with a great deal of snout nudging, bumping, and touching on head and neck.

While the crocodilian's image as a toothy-jawed predator is well-deserved (and even this comparatively meek-mouthed Indian gavial's hundred razor-sharp teeth slice through the water to trap passing fish), those mouths are made for singing as well. As a prelude to mating the male alligator, for example, performs a little water concert, sending out from somewhere in the center of his body powerful subsonic signals that can travel miles across still water. A female detecting them rushes to the male and puts her snout on his chin. Closing her eyes, she seems to yield to the experience of the vibration. But the choice of male is hers; if an unwanted suitor approaches she makes mewing sounds that attract other males. Mating begins with two crocodilians parallel but in opposite directions. The first turns, riding up on the other's head, forcing it underwater. Though eventually they align, copulation is made difficult by the location of both vents on the undersides of their tails, so that the male must clasp the female with his forelegs, roll to his side, and slide partially beneath her. In thirty seconds it is over—rapid, compared to most reptiles.

Despite their reputation as ruthless predators, wolves are the model mates.

ALPHA AND OTHERS

Led by an "alpha" couple, male and female, the wolf pack consists of an orderly progression of lesser wolves who are their siblings or offspring. With rank comes privileges. As the breeding season approaches in the spring, tempers fray. Females get a bit edgy, and males circle about eyeing them. But only one couple actually mates—and it is the king and queen of the pack. There is a biological reason for it; their pups do not have to compete for food, and they have the additional advantage of aunts and uncles to care for them. Once mated to the alpha male, the alpha female may have relations with the other males. This has the pleasant side benefit of keeping the males contented and confusing the issue of the pups' parenthood. The alpha male and female mate with ceremony. They exchange affectionate licks, and he mounts her. As their excitement swells, the male pivots and faces the rear, and for twenty minutes they stay in this amatory embrace. The rest of the pack watch, resigning themselves to their vicarious role, which will not change until the alpha couple die or grow too old to mate.

*Proof positive
that sex makes life
complicated, the
peacock struggles
along the forest
floor dragging his
immense regalia
of tail.*

VANITY'S EYE

Peacocks reached Europe about the time of Alexander the Great, and ever since, western naturalists and moralists have used the male with his gold, green, and white feathers as the symbol of vanity. Leonardo da Vinci noted in his Beastiarium that "the peacock is always contemplating the beauty of its tail, spreading it out in the form of a wheel and attracting by its cries the attention of animals." We know now that the peacock spreads his tail for one reason, and it is sexual: to catch a peahen. The male presents a peahen with an array of elongated tail feathers, each surmounted by a glowing round "ocellus," or eye; he then vibrates his tail to suggest a great deal more movement than is actually involved. The tail is a vast chorus of sexual sign stimuli. Rotating, he turns his side to her; if she is truly interested she must run around so the eyes on his tail feathers are before her. The male rattles his feathers and the love test goes on and on till the hen is sufficiently overwhelmed, and crouches invitingly to be mounted.

Zalophus californianus, or the California sea lion, can be found during the mating season along the California coast, as far south as the Galápagos, and as far west as Japan.

GENTLE GESTURES

The sea lion's procreative ability can only be called "abundant," as populations reach record proportions. Living in a herd with a dominant male and about fifteen females, the sea lion breeds every May to June, when after a pregnancy of a full year the female gives birth to a single brown pup. Two hours later (no rest for the weary) the call to mate sounds, and a cacophony of noisy barks ensues, often accompanied by biting and tumbling. The sea lion mates either on land or in the waves. Aquatic sex takes a skillful skipper, and is complicated by the female's constant swimming movement and her habit of rolling over. To master the seduction, the male grasps the female on her head, nose, or chin. Once her back rests against his belly, he turns the pair of them so she is above him. His head is completely submerged, but his chest and abdomen are bowed up high out of the water. In between couplings, the lord of the harem patrols the shore back and forth all day long, barking when he surfaces.

Love among the turtles (despite their hard, unprepossessing shell) is a tender affair, given the animal's clumsiness. When a male meets a female he swims slowly toward her till they nearly touch. After a series of quivering movements with forelegs, heads stretch forward and then withdraw as excitement mounts. When the dance has worked its magic she drops to the bottom of the water and extends her tail. The male hastily clambers onto her back, drops his own tail, and then introduces his organ to the female's cloaca; there they remain for hours. For the female Galápagos tortoise who withholds her favors, the male may bang on her shell in protest. If she still proves too coy, the male's technique is to snap at her legs or head. Since at mating time she is especially fat, she reacts by withdrawing her head, whereupon her hind end emerges. The male can mate only when the female plainly tells him she is ready. Once mounted, the male uses the spiny tips of his tail to stimulate her genitals, until she extends her hind end. Some tortoises also sing to each other, with babylike aah-aahing cries, while the male moves his head left and right in rhythm.

Turtles and tortoises embody much of the history of sexual union, since the primitive form of the mammalian penis originated with their ancestors.

HARD KNOCKS

LODGE FELLOWS

*Male nest building
is rare among
mammals, but
beaver couples
cooperate in
building dams and
in collecting the
food necessary
to survive winter.*

Drifting along the surface of a stream, a couple of beavers embrace, forelegs locked around each other, breast to breast. Beavers choose each other as adolescents and live together at a parent's home for at least six months before they are sexually mature enough to take courtship to its logical conclusion. When the time is ripe, and with a great deal of splashing, the male turns the female on her back, clasps her firmly around the neck and body with front and hind feet—and is finished copulating in three minutes. Afterward, the supportive and sociable family pitches in to help the new couple build their first home. No residence in the animal kingdom elicits more wonder than the beaver's impregnable lodge. A one-room dwelling large enough to hold a man is made with sticks, stone, mud, and logs, with a formal entrance. The female helps build the lodge, but once installed, and having borne her first litter, lets the male handle all future repairs. Interestingly, beavers (like all animals that stay paired for more than one season) tend to be sexually monomorphic; that is, male and female are about the same size, shape, and weight, and look virtually identical.

PRIDE OF PLACE

Though most felines are solitary creatures, lions live in communal prides; females form the core, and cubs and adult males come and go.

The lion's noble, tawney head and wide-eyed gaze have made him not only king of the beasts but a deity among the ancient Egyptians, a heraldic symbol among the Europeans, and a totem among African tribes. Part of the legend has to do with the "queen's" sexual appetite when in heat: in a period of sixty hours one lioness was recorded mating 170 times, and when one exhausted male gave up, another male took his place. In the courtship game it is the female who sets the rules. The lioness circles the male, gives him her scent, flicks her tail in his face, and walks away. He follows her and they mate for a few seconds. Then they rest for a few moments and start again, and again—and every time the lioness initiates the ritual. All this rampant activity takes place within a formal social life. Females in a pride tend to be related and even take turns nursing one another's cubs. Four-year-old males are driven out (which prevents them from mating with their mothers and sisters) and lead a nomadic existence until they are strong enough to dispossess a ruling male and assume his sexual responsibilities.

46

If the stallion dies, the mares still stay together, moving collectively into the harem of another stallion. Males without harems live in peaceable bachelor groups, whose encounters are marked by an ornate welcoming ceremony of stretching necks forward, sniffing each other's muzzles, and assuming the "greeting face": ears tipped forward, lips retracted, chewing on air. Sex adds some tensions to the quiet habits of the zebra. When a young female first comes into heat, every stallion in the area makes a try at abducting her. Her father vigorously chases off one only to discover a dozen more sidling up. Eventually hours of rebuffing suitors wear him out, and off she marches. But the courtship is not over: she does not allow the stallion to mount her, and if he is not attentive she may be abducted again—it can happen several times before she settles down. If he has a harem, he has to defend this new female from his wives' initial aggression, and if he manages to keep her it may be six months before they copulate and a year before she is fertile—a curious delaying mechanism that ensures her readiness for motherhood and a supportive family circle.

The core of plains zebra society is a stallion with mares and foals, and cementing these bonds are female friendships that last for life.

STABLE TIES

49

Like some immense,
smooth, and hairless
submarine, the hippo
closes his slitlike
nostrils, folds down
his ears, and
descends to the river
bottom in rings
of soundless ripples.

LOVE IN THE MUD

The African hippo's massive slate-brown, three-ton body is encased in a sleek epidermis that acts as a wick to allow the transfer of water. Found singly, in pairs, or in larger groups of mud-wallowers splashing in concert, the hippo is rarely violent, establishing its territory instead by using bodily excretions as signposts. To ward off rivals that do appear, hippos hold yawning contests; bulls gape aggressively when territory is threatened. If this fails to impress, dung scattering, forward rushes and dives, water blowing through the nostrils, water fights, and staccato grunts follow, until one male lowers his head in submission. Territorial encounters make for a vaudeville ritual: males stop, stare, present their rears, defecate at each other, and then (point made) waddle away. Breeding, which can occur at any time of the year once hippos become sexually mature at five or six, brings out a tigerish streak. During a three-day rut a bull may habitually use his tusklike teeth as weapons to establish dominance. When the opportunity for hour-long copulation results, the female submerges, her tightly shut eyes and relaxed bubble-blowing conveying a distinct impression of pleasure.

*All bears show
a propensity for
solitude, but the
polar bear is even
more of a hermit
by inclination.*

ARCTIC NIGHTS

Sea ice has no boundaries, and so the heavy-clawed emperors of the ice give each other wide berth. Even the polar bear must socialize, however, in order to produce new bears. In the late spring, when blankets of vapor rise from the newly melting pools, the female comes into heat, and her scent wafting across the ice sheets lures a half-dozen males to follow. She leads them on a merry chase until finally only one male bear still follows at a discrete distance. Then with much bobbing of heads and circling, the love duet begins. The female pauses now and then to perfume the snow with urine. She might allow some intimacy, a lingering sniff at her crotch, a quick nuzzle, and then rush away. Mating is thought to be tumultuous, judging from the churned-up snow left behind and the occasional broken penis bone that turns up in an Eskimo hunter's catch. During this time, the male defends the female against new arrivals (though if he is unlucky he may lose her to a stronger mate). After a few weeks together, they drift apart. Her egg will float for months in a dormant state, then implant itself in her womb that autumn for a foal in spring.

For cave-dwelling North American bats, most of the year is devoted to sexually segregated hibernation, and courtship has to be packed into a few active autumnal weeks. The female bat releases an odor from throat or rear and, catching a whiff, the male comes purring and chattering alongside. A weird sign language of thumbs, forearms, and wings finally leads to an embrace, upside down in her ceiling niche. The grotesque-looking male hammer-headed bat sets up house in the African rainforest, underneath the dense jungle canopy, where he flaps his wings and honks for passing females. When a male spots a potential mate he adds a rakish staccato buzz. Females may visit up to six males a night (hovering critically to compare their performances) before deciding on a mate. Male Gambian epauletted bats gather at dusk and spend the evenings defending their sites. When the females arrive, near midnight, the males unfurl tufts of white hair from shoulder pockets thought to contain perfumes, which are wafted into the night by his gently flapping wings, luring a mate. By three in the morning, a hundred thousand wing beats later, the exhausted males retire.

One of nature's more curious sexual displays is the upside-down mating of the only mammal that flies, the bat.

SEX ON THE WING

A secret language used by three-quarters of all species in the animal kingdom is the chemical language of pheromones.

STINK FIGHTS

"Pheromone" is a term meaning in ancient Greek "transference of excitement," though not all pheromones are related to the excitation of courtship, and fewer still serve as sexual attractants. Some identify the individual's sex or rank in a group. Brown lemurs, who live in troops of up to twenty individuals among rocky caves and in wooded areas of Madagascar and the Comoro Islands, use them as territorial markers on branches and trees; or sometimes, as agents of attack. In "stink fights" between rival ring-tailed males, combatants rub the hormones secreted by their wrist glands onto their tails, which they wave menacingly at each other much like long swords. Stink-fight season precedes breeding season, twice a year, and is a time of social upheaval among the lemurs, marked by a discordant symphony of piercing whistles, loud shrieks, and (when breeding) pleasurable grunts that continues until new orders of dominance are established.

In a foam nest

formed of bubbles

given tensile

strength by the

fishes' saliva, male

mouthbrooders

lure females by

ceremonial kisses.

KISSING CONTESTS

Love and hate are indistinguishable in the early stages of sexual bonding (and even two males may lock labia aggressively). First the male and then the female mouthbrooder grips the other's lips for up to forty seconds, a kissing contest of such vigor that skin sometimes rips off, dangling from their mouths. This love play has the effect of persuading the female to release her eggs. The mates then guard the eggs and, later, the hatched offspring—using their mouths to scoop up any precious progeny who try to escape too soon from parental custody, spitting them back into the nest. When danger threatens, the mother's or father's mouth can provide a sanctuary for the hatchlings: hence the descriptive name.

*Like a reminder
of some prehistoric
ice age, the
duckbilled platypus
is said to descend
from an obscure
mammalian line
150 million
years old.*

THE PARADOX OF THE PLATYPUS

First known to western scientists in 1798, the rarefied platypus has a wide, flat bill and webbed feet that are certainly ducklike, but the female's reproductive system is decidedly reptilian. It uses a single orifice, called a cloaca, for both excretion and reproduction. But the platypus's cloaca actually is divided—sperm has a separate channel—and the male's penis is forked to match the female's fork-shaped vagina. Like birds and reptiles the platypus lays eggs, but the wide tail is like a beaver's, covered by shiny brown fur, and the female nurses her young like all mammals. A loner by temperament, the platypus begins the search for a mate in summer, and during the courting session engages in some eccentric rituals. The male, for example, swims around and around with the female's tail in his mouth. While they nuzzle with their exquisitely sensitive bills, the female has to avoid entangling herself in the male's hind feet. There he has a sharp, hollow spur loaded with a venom that is designed for territorial fights with rival males, and which (ironically for the danger they present her) only activate during mating season.

THE HAREM MASTERS

Nowhere is the polygamist's burden more weighty than among the elephant seals, whose long trunklike noses have earned them their name.

In no other animal is the sexes' size ratio more dramatic; the bull may weigh upward of twelve hundred pounds while his consorts rarely exceed six hundred. The lives of dominant bulls are characterized by transient glories. In his prime, one lone bull may claim a harem of fifty females. He will go without food for three months to devote his entire efforts to copulating, but will stop his lovemaking on a dime if he should spot another bull trying to inch closer to his domain. When the males first arrive at the beach, tests of strength and will are the order of the day. The beach is red streaked by the time that fighters turn and flee. Dominance is established; males fan out from the strongest bull in descending order. Females arrive a few weeks later to be herded ashore by their lords. The females quickly give birth to the pups conceived the previous year and, barely weeks after, the call to action sounds as a male throws a flipper over a female and rolls her onto her back. If she resists, by whacking her flippers at the male's penis or dashing sand in his face, he tries to pin her down. Eventually they come to some agreement; or else he leaves her for a more receptive mate.

Aerobically draining
serenades by these
Australian tree
frogs stimulate both
the male singer
and the listening
female.

AN AMPHIBIAN CHORUS

Large males, calling from tree branches in the dense rainforest, use their longer vocal cords and softer croaks to readily attract females—while small males, hearing a deep croak, desist, sensing futility. Among common frogs, males stay in the breeding area for a full three weeks, females for a mere three days. Competition is intense, as wily males try to intercept partners before they reach the mating area. Encountering a female, a male jumps on her back and clasps her under the forelegs in a position called "amplexus." Other males try to jump on, with the first rider using his strong hind legs to kick them away. Soon a large ball of struggling males is smothering the unfortunate female (a few do die of asphyxiation). Nevertheless the wrestling match is not yet over. Since male frogs lack a penis, they must wait until the female makes up her mind to release the eggs; her abdominal contractions signal him to release his sperm at the same time. The tension-filled ride and prolonged squeezing make frog sex last for up to twelve hours—among the longest, ounce for ounce, in the animal kingdom.

A CONICAL OFFERING

The Urodela family—of newts and salamanders— are mute in love, but make up for silence with action.

In a surprisingly ornate embrace, the male red-spotted newt nuzzles his head back and forth against his mate's, slapping his tail against her body. Their love play goes on for a few hours with the action rising to a crescendo, the male shaking and the female twisting in agitation. After each wild outburst, the steadying caressing begins again: the rubbing of heads back and forth, the rhythmic tail-slapping. Then the male crawls out on land with a waddling gait; the female follows. He contorts himself, placing on the ground a cone-shaped ball of sperm wrapped in jelly. With a flick of her tail, she advances and lowers her body down. The sperm sac is perfectly positioned and she sucks it up into her cloaca, consummation completed. But, if she has changed her mind, she devours the cone instead. The feckless male can only hope that his offering is graciously accepted.

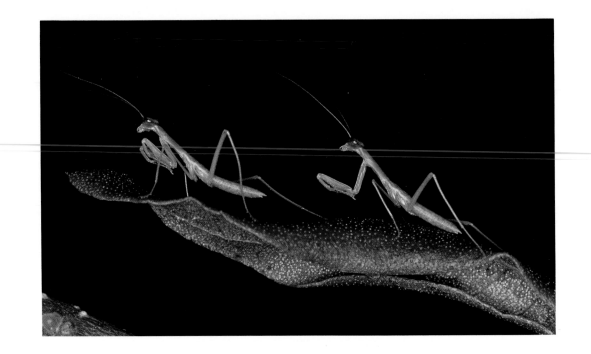

The saintly bearing,
with forelimbs held
upward in the
traditional posture of
devout supplication,
has given the
praying mantis its
evocative name.

CANNIBAL COPULATION

The ancient Greeks attributed supernatural powers to the mantis, while Moslems believed the position assumed always faced Mecca. But those delicate forelimbs are actually murderous weapons, with the sharp, serrated edges of a jackknife. The female of this species is more voracious than the black widow spider, trying to consume her mate before, during, or after copulation. The male has one slight advantage: she is nearsighted—so he approaches her stealthily, risking that she could turn and suddenly bite off his head. Even if that happens his sex drive is so strong, that though his top half is missing, his bottom half remains inflamed and mounts to copulate while she munches on his head. Afterward the decapitated male slumps to the ground and she consumes the rest of him. There is more to the decapitation than mere cannibalism, for the brain of the male apparently tends to inhibit copulation, an activity controlled by a nervous center in the abdomen of the insect. By beheading her mate, the female is actually enabling his performance of the sex act.

Fluttering on summer nights, moths display the evolutionary discovery that the light protects them from their predator, the dark-loving bat.

LIGHT SIDE OF THE MOON

By the light of day, moths' genius for camouflage extends to their bodily tissue. All spring long they eat and eat, becoming by summer the colors of the leaves and twigs they so ravenously consume. To help ensure the cycle of life, their coloring also carries some deception, for birds may think twice about attacking snakes, and the wingtip patterns of numerous moths evoke the skin patterns of venomous species of banded serpents. Such mimicry is also characteristic of other insects—butterflies, plant hoppers, water striders, and, also, caterpillars—sometimes to a startling degree. Meanwhile, the short-lived but remarkable saturnid male moth uses his sense of smell to detect a mate miles away, and even at these extreme distances he can determine if a given female is a virgin. Using enormously enlarged antennae containing thousands of sensory cells, he flies upwind by the light of the moon until he is able to locate the volatile secretions dispersed on her fluttering wings.

LEKS OF LOVE

"Lekking" comes from the old English word for play and describes the sage grouse mating system, by which the "men" distinguish themselves from the "boys."

Like teenage boys at a Texas social, the sage grouse males lounge around together in the brush (at the lek) waiting for females to wander by. While there, they challenge each other: strutting their cock feathers, ruffling their necks, preening, and making a popping noise by blowing air out of their esophageal sacs. They compete fiercely for the best front-and-center territories, where their elaborate plumage will be most visible to prospective mates. When females fly into the lek a few weeks into the mating season, the party starts and a mad frenzy of lekking display begins. But the real action, sadly for the boys, falls to a few dominant males; only ten percent get to perform ninety percent of the mating. To add insult to injury, prowess is demonstrated in full view of the lek, where these main males have staked out their turf. The females then begin the task of producing and rearing their young all alone. The beauty contest subsides; the dejected suitors disband.

In addition to their virtually instantaneous impregnation, the hares of the genus Lepus have some notable peculiarities. The snowshoe hare male, for example, has a penis that is pale white before the breeding season, blending in nicely with his snowy winter coat. But just before the period of heat begins it blushes red at the tip, with the rosy color slowly spreading to the entire penis—certain to attract special attention from all females. Only the wiliest, strongest, and most dexterous hare males will mate with most of the females. Contestants stand erect on the tiptoes of their hind feet and box furiously. The only sound is the thudding of their rapid-fire blows, and whenever the opportunity presents, either hare may "kick-box" with the hind feet—a move that can disembowel the rival. The winner established, copulation soon follows, with the same brutal roughhouse tactics: the male seizes the fur on his mate's neck or sinks his teeth into her and hangs on for the (mercifully short) duration.

GO FORTH AND MULTIPLY

"Breeding like rabbits" (or its cruder, vernacular equivalent) has become a stock expression for fecundity.

When you say
"giraffe" (the
name comes from
the Arabic zarafah)
you think "neck,"
the longest in the
animal kingdom.

THE SEVEN-VERTEBRAE ADVANTAGE

A true wonder of the animal world, paraded in the Coliseum by Julius Caesar, giraffes are not everyone's idea of bonny with their bulging eyes, hairy mouths, and eighteen-inch tongues. They also have monstrous (thirty-pound) hearts and equally giant-sized appetites, each beast consuming 120 pounds of greenery a day. The neck is integral to giraffe sexuality. A male's typical feeding stance is with head and neck fully outstretched to reach about nineteen feet, up into the woodland tree canopy. Females, in marked contrast, curl their necks over, chewing at body or knee height. When males confront each other, they "stand tall"—and the longest neck wins. Or they do some "necking," ritualized fighting indulged in to decide dominance, a little like arm wrestling in humans. But for both sexes this seven-vertebrae extender guarantees a nutrient-rich diet, which in turn ensures that giraffes can breed all year long.

In deciding on a mate, female fairy terns put males through a rigorous practical test—courtship feeding.

GLITTERING GIFTS

In the animal world as in the human, there are the flashy here-today, gone-tomorrow males and the solid, dependable types who shoulder the burden. As fairy-tern courtship begins the male flies around showing a choice morsel of glittering mackerel to prospective partners, seemingly reluctant to give up his hard-won prize. Soon the field narrows, as females scrutinize males to choose the best provider. A mutual interest develops and a male alights before a female and offers his fish as a gift. Once she accepts, the two fly off together. When they land, the female must again accept the fish from the male, as though to seal their alliance. As a relationship develops, a male more and more readily brings home victuals and lays them at his partner's feet. The nutritional importance of this is obvious—the more food he supplies, the more eggs she lays, and the healthier, stronger, and more successful their young.

78

ACKNOWLEDGMENTS

Grateful thanks to Lala Herrero Salas, whose tireless research provided the raw material in the early stages of the project. We would also like to thank Vanessa Ryan for her elegant design and endless grace under pressure. Many thanks also to friends and colleagues for their knowledge, time, and patience in the research process, including Les Kaufman, Chief Scientist, Edgerton Research Lab, New England Aquarium, for his ruthless and peerless vetting of all the material here; Gonzalo Escuder of New York University; Bill Perry from National Geographic; Tim Harris from NHPA; Ben Rose from The National Zoo; Douglas B. Smith from Boston Museum of Science; Bill Holmstrom, Jamie James, Steve Johnson, Peter Taylor and Roseanne Thiemann from Wildlife Conservation International at the New York Zoological Society; Dennis Thoney and Paul Sieswerda from W.C.I. at the New York Aquarium; Jonathan David of Tulip Films; and Andy Karsch of Longfellow Pictures. Very special thanks to Caroline Herter of Chronicle Books, as well as Charlotte Stone, Carey Charlesworth, and Fonda Duvanel, who took such a keen interest in this project and without whose many suggestions and unwavering enthusiasm this book would have hibernated forever.

PICTURE CREDITS